*To the cherished memory of my father, Estlee Ted Mercer,
and to the good folks of Ambrose, Georgia, who raised
him to become a great American soldier. —P.M.*

*To John, Rod, and Rob, who constantly inspire
me to live a life beyond myself. —R.M.*

Text copyright © 2007 by Peggy Mercer
Illustrations copyright © 2007 by Ron Mazellan
All rights reserved
CIP Data is available
Published in the United States in 2007
by Handprint Books
413 Sixth Avenue
Brooklyn, NY 11215
www.handprintbooks.com
First Edition
Design by Rianna Riegelman
Printed in China
ISBN-13: 978-1-59354-192-7
ISBN-10: 1-59354-192-9
2 4 6 8 10 9 7 5 3 1

To Axel — and Malena and Lily —
Love, Grandma Jeannie xo xo xo

There Come a Soldier

BY **Peggy Mercer**

ILLUSTRATED BY **Ron Mazellan**

HANDPRINT BOOKS  BROOKLYN, NEW YORK

THE TALL MAN in the olive-drab uniform yelled,
"Who will fight for his country, brave and true?"
Papa shouted, "I will, sir!"

For he was a boy once, who
roamed the banks of Wiggins Creek.
He scouted those deep dark waters
where snapping turtles hid. Papa
waded, chest-deep, into the creek
and led two brothers, three sisters,
and a girl named Ruthie to the other side.

One day, the tall man in the olive-drab uniform yelled, "Who will jump from an airplane?" Papa shouted, "I will, sir!"

For he was a boy once, who loved jumping
from a hayloft on a farm in Ambrose, Georgia.
He egged on his brothers and sisters and Ruthie,
too, although it took a right smart of coaxing.

Now Papa was a paratrooper.
He practiced jumping from high
towers and somersaulting when he hit
the ground. He ran fast for the wind
could blow parachutes away. He learned
to collapse the parachute and stow it safely.

   One day, Papa packed a green duffel
bag and spit-shined his army boots.
He crossed the ocean on a great ship,
the *Queen Elizabeth*.

In England, Papa crowded into a C-47.
Soon, the jumpmaster commanded loudly,
"Get ready! Stand up! Hook up!"
Papa shouted, "Yes, sir!"

For he was a boy once, swinging on a knotty
vine on the dam of a hog wallow. Papa's two
brothers and three sisters and Ruthie chanted,
"Come on, it ain't nothin' but a old killer hog!"
And Papa yelled "Geronimoooo!"
and swung up and over the
snarling hog.

Now Papa was the first paratrooper in the door of the airplane. On the wing, the red light turned green for go! Papa jumped far and fast, counting, "One thousand, two thousand, three thousand!" And on "three thousand," his parachute opened.

Papa dropped into the Ardennes Forest. When all the parachutes were buried and every man was accounted for, Papa dug his foxhole. He wrote a letter home, in cursive with a number-two pencil:

Dear Ruthie,
  I've been busy jumping out of airplanes behind enemy lines. These folks have put me in charge of a whole pile of other soldiers. Ain't that something? Well, sugar pie, it's time for my C-rations.

And it's time, he thought but did not write, to turn to the certain job ahead.

For he was a boy once, plowing old Red and
Gray sunup till sundown in the Georgia fields.
Gee!—go right—and Haw!—go left. Papa
plowed every row on every acre, and it was
known far and wide, Papa finished every
row he ever started.

Now, a good ways before dawn,
Papa climbed out of the foxhole.
He motioned, trying hard to count
the shadows of every paratrooper.
   The icy wind was brutal, and snow
blinded Papa, but the soldiers moved
forward. They fell and got up. They got
lost and got found. They ducked gunfire.
Day became afternoon, and as night
spread over them, they were separated.
   I am just a country boy, Papa told himself,
and I may perish in this war where nobody
knows me. Yet, strangely, that very thought
filled him fresh with grit.

For he was a boy once, rising 'fore the rooster crowed to work in the Georgia fields. Wishful thinking and hurting bones had not stood in cotton's way. And by no small miracle the backbreaking work had not killed him then, or his two brothers and three sisters, or Ruthie.

Now Papa stopped on a hill. He brushed
the ice from his eyelashes. In the valley
below was the market town of Bastogne
and the battle Papa had come for.

And at the very edge of the town stood
a stone barn. Papa's hands shook, and
though he could not recollect ever being
so weary, he knew this much: With just a
little rest, he could hang on forever!

For he was a boy once, caught
in a summer storm on the Satilla River.
Lightning zapped and zinged and the tossing
waters flipped the canoe. For hours on end
Papa and his two brothers clung to the sides.
At last the storm stopped and they swam to shore.

Now Papa ran through a firefight. He jumped and dodged and lead hit his leg and still Papa raced. He jumped over barbed wire, twisted, hunkered down, crouched, and came closer to the barn. Closer! Papa ducked inside.

The barn stank of animal dung, old ashes, and mold. Part of a wall was crumbled, and high above pigeons wobbled back and forth on rafters. Outside, gunfire rattled the night.

Hidden in the shadows, Papa
sagged against a wall and slid down.
He squatted and rubbed his leg. His
eyelids drooped and suddenly popped open.
 Across the barn, there come a soldier!
The soldier slinked, inched, crept toward Papa.
Papa pressed his back to the wall and bit his
tongue. He knew a thing or two about holding still.

For he was a boy once, run up a live oak
tree by a black bear after honey. Papa set
to thinking he'd stay high and dry forever.
But after the very longest while, the old
bear got bored and meandered away.

Now Papa held still as a tombstone. The soldier moved closer and stopped. Papa could not see if the soldier was us or them. But in his heart he knew it was them. The soldier slid down beside Papa. Their shoulders touched and held steady. And while Papa's troubled heart was figuring on what to do, something beckoned to him from long ago.

For he was a boy once, whose mama had gathered her young'uns on pallets in their sharecropper's shack. In the suddenly mean Georgia winter, Papa's family had warmed him better than a blanket. And in the pale lantern glow, his mama had leaned close and told them this gift,

"Always be a brother."

Through the jagged rafters above,
something gleamed—a ray of light, so faint
it seemed from a faraway candle. Yet from it spun
a ribbon of gold past the pigeons and onto the floor
where it formed a wide and perfect ring.

And in the ring poked the toes of many soldier's boots!
Heat flowed shoulder to shoulder to shoulder as the soldiers
huddled together against this winter, against this war.

Before first light, Papa
slipped from the barn.
Behind him, soldiers quietly
emerged into the dawn,
heads down, through holes
and from windows. Papa
crawled through snowdrifts,
scrambling, searching,
and at last finding his men.

In a few days' time Papa had fought in the Battle of the Bulge and was in someways a hero.

When the paratroopers were relieved by ground troops, Papa was flown to the United States to a hospital.

He was stitched up—not so nice and easy—by an army doctor. All he asked for was a number-two pencil, so he could write this letter in cursive:

Dear Ruthie,
I've been wounded and these folks ain't gonna let me fight no more.
I'm comin' home.

The locomotive shuddered to a stop where the roads crossed in Ambrose, Georgia. Dogs darted at the train wheels, barking like all get out. Ladies leaned out their open windows and some ran outside, waving tiny flags. Grannies clapped from rocking chairs, and young'uns peeked around porch posts. Men stopped plowing and took off their hats.

Papa got down from the train. He hobbled to Ruthie and handed her a golden heart on a purple ribbon. She flung her arms around Papa and someone blew a bugle.

Men boxed Papa's arm and said, "'At boy's a hero!" and near about everybody there cried enough tears to make Wiggins Creek a river.

Papa stood there just
swarmed by all those
good folks. And although
his mouth would not say
words, in Papa's heart was this:
I heard y'all call me from a long ways off.

For he was a boy once, shaping memories like friends in a circle, hand in hand. And Papa found this: No matter how far a boy might go, the circle goes. No matter how strong the cold wind blows, the circle holds. And when enemies came, Papa heard from the memory-friends, *"Let 'em in."*